MW01042039

WINKLE
IN THE
LUNCHROOM

Suzanne Caron

To order additional copies of this book, contact:
Xlibris
1-888-795-4274
www.Xlibris.com
Orders@Xlibris.com

ISBN: Softcover   978-1-7960-7146-7
       EBook   978-1-7960-7145-0

Print information available on the last page

Rev. date: 11/13/2019

To George, Holland, Melody and Sawyer,

Remember that you can do anything you set your mind to. Keep on reaching for your dreams. It's not always easy, but you all have the ability to succeed!

 Love, YIa-Yia

My name is Winkle from Willow Woods. I live inside the hollow of a wispy willow tree with my family Screech and Echo.

Each morning, I zip to Willow School as fast as I can.
I like being in my classroom.

But I hate, hate, hate the lunchroom!
Why?
I SIT ALL BY MYSELF AT THE LUNCH
TABLE! Nobody sits with me.

I am friendly. I say Hi and Please and Thank you even when I don't feel like it.

I wonder why I am alone. I stare into my lunch box so that others will not see that I am trying not to cry.

One afternoon, I fly home and, without hooting a word, I go straight to my bedroom. I do not want to eat my snack. I am not hungry. I slam my door so hard that my lamp falls off my night stand. I plop myself on my bed, hiding my face in the blankets.

Screech and Echo slowly crack open my door and take a peek. I look up at them, and they see my long face. (By the way, that means sad looking).

"Winkle, what is the matter? ", Echo asked. "You seem to be very upset about something".

I mumble, "Nobody ever sits with me during lunch. When I try to sit next to someone, they go and sit somewhere else. It makes my heart hurt and my eyes wet."

Screech and Echo quietly listen.
Echo speaks softly, "Thank you for
sharing this with us, Winkle. We
will see if we can help".
Then Screech kisses me on my pointy
little ear, and it tickles. I try real
hard not to smile, but I can't help
it. I do feel a teensy bit better.

The next day, I fly to school as usual. You will never guess what happens! Sage, my teacher, reads a book to the class about an owl that felt invisible because no one paid attention to it.

All of a sudden I feel like a super hero. I hope it is ok for a super hero to be scared because I can't stop my skinny legs from shaking or my heart from beating like a drum.

But I must do this.
I raise my wing. The teacher says,
"Yes, Winkle?" "May I say something
to the class?"
Teacher Sage smiles and gives me
the thumbs up. (That means ok.)

Now I feel brave and I speak. "I feel invisible like the owl in the story. It hurts my feelings when no one sits next to me during lunch. It makes me a bit mad too, because I treat you all kindly and I do not think I should be treated like this."
The room is very quiet.

Sandy flaps her wing, "I feel invisible too sometimes. Winkle, I will sit with you. I never meant to hurt your feelings".
I smile from ear to ear. I really do!

A furry paw is raised. "I want to sit with you too!"
Then another, and another!

What a day!

Winkle's advice: Your voice is your super hero power. Use it. Tell a grown up what is bothering you. Sometimes you have to tell more than one. Echo called Teacher Sage. She read the book. Everyone shared their feelings. Never forget that you deserve to be loved and happy!

CPSIA information can be obtained
at www.ICGtesting.com
Printed in the USA
BVHW021120120120
569240BV00002B/2/P